I'LL JUST WAIT

S E A S O N   1

A NOVEL/SCREENPLAY
BY
A R E V A   D E N I S E   N E E L Y

I'LL JUST WAIT   SEASON 1   AREVA DENISE NEELY

I'LL JUST WAIT

(SEASON 1)

A NOVEL/SCREENPLAY WRITTEN BY

Areva Denise Neely

I'LL JUST WAIT

A NOVEL/SCREENPLAY WRITTEN BY

AREVA DENISE NEELY

Scripture quotations are from various versions of the Holy Bible.

For additional information, please contact:
IllJustWait25@gmail.com

For information about special discounts for bulk purchases please contact the Special Sales Department
Library of Congress Cataloging-in Publication Data
For additional information, please contact:
(951) 796-0282

For information about special discounts for bulk purchases please contact the Special Sales Department at IllJustWait25@gmail.com

Library of Congress Cataloging-in Publication Data
Areva Denise Neely

Published by Executive Business Writing
Moreno Valley, CA 92552
(951)488-7634
https://www.executivebusinesswriting.com
executivebusinesswriting@gmail.com

Edited by Julie Boney
JB Editing Solutions
www.jb-editingsolutions.com

Graphics by Tracy Spencer
Legacy Media, LLC
Moreno Valley, CA 92552

TABLE OF CONTENTS

FOREWORD

Wait: To stay where one is or delay action until a particular time or until something else happens.

Areva has demonstrated the true definition of walking in faith, and trusting in God's timing. Oftentimes people get so impatient with what the future holds, or reaching a certain goal, that they fail to realize what God has planned for us, and will happen... in His timing.

I'll Just Wait will help you in navigating life's trials when you want something so bad, but it's not the right time. Areva exemplifies what it means to be a humble Christian who diligently works to please God and share His love. It is no secret that Areva has been hurt, mistreated, and misunderstood. Nevertheless, she has held on to God's promise and calling over her life. *I'll Just Wait* is a story of trusting in God's timing, even when we don't understand why it's not happening now.

Shaleta Wilkinson

Foreword

ACKNOWLEDGEMENTS

I want to acknowledge all the young women who are still saving themselves for marriage, and those who are committing to celibacy.

To my parents, siblings, nieces, and nephews, thank you for always supporting me!

Acknowledgements

DEDICATION

This book is dedicated to my cousin, Lotasha Crosby Carver, who passed away of pancreatic cancer in November of 2019. She was literally one of my biggest fans in everything that I did or thought of doing!

I love and miss you, and thank you for always believing in me! Loving you, Tasha, was so easy to do because of all the love God put in you! Your warm hugs, kisses, and nicknames, made us laugh even when you were in pain.

Your love was unconditional and more selfless than my words can express. You were overprotective because your love was so strong, and truly, one of the best. You would definitely throw down if someone came at any of your family wrong!

Tasha, you meant everything to me. In the last moments I got to spend with you, you said to me, "Areva, I was in prayer for you to stay in your lane and do ministry. You are born to be different. Everything God has put inside of you, and every dream and idea will come to pass. Just stay in your lane. You're not like everybody else. Remember, I'm always one of your biggest fans forever." She was an amazing woman inside and out!

Dedication

Salvation is what we have. I (we) can have peace of mind knowing without a doubt you're resting in Heaven with Jesus. Tasha, you're most likely throwing down some food and Sangria with grandma and grandpa while watching this beautiful dedication to you.

I am honored to be your little cousin/sibling; to have known you was sincerely a privilege. I will never ever forget all you did for me as a little girl, teenager, and adult.

You were definitely the realist! I can genuinely say you spoke truth and had no problem telling anyone to their face how you felt, and I respect you for that!

Admirable faith you had, especially seeing you fight and trust God during your pain and telling others to do the same. Lotasha, I love you and I'm going to miss you!

Your Reever, Pooh, and Boo forever!

INTRODUCTION

You are getting ready to go through a TV series about a young woman who is saving herself until marriage. Not usual for this modern-day way of thinking, right? So, grab some junk food because you're going to encounter some close calls, and some difficult decisions.

When you do not keep God in the center of your relationships, that is what your life will feel like — a TV series. Welcome to Season 1.

PS...

Remember, you're worth more and definitely worth the wait.

Introduction

PILOT

Hello ladies.

My name is Areva Denise Neely. First and foremost, you are an incredible woman! Better yet, you were written about 2000 years ago, in the canons.

Proverbs 3:15: *"She is more precious than rubies: and all the things you can desire are not to be compared to her."*

So, my questions to you are: How valuable are you? Do you think you're worth the wait? I am here to tell you you're worth the wait and you are so valuable. You are not beautiful just on the outside but the inside as well. I hope you enjoy this show. I hope it makes you realize how valuable you are!

Pilot

Episode 1: SPIRIT IS WILLING, FLESH IS WEAK

Matthew 26:41:*"Watch and pray that you may not enter into temptation. The spirit indeed is willing, but the flesh is weak."*

It was a cold winter December night in San Diego, California, in 2015. Usually, the basic climate features are hot, sunny, and dry summers. Hence they are famous for their miles and miles of white-sand beaches and amazing weather. However, December is the coldest month, overall, for San Diego.

Chloe, fresh out of a hot shower, wrapped in a hammam Turkish beige towel, her hair in a pink bonnet, was feeling exhausted from a long day of her last semester of pediatric residency. She sits down on her queen-size bed, which has a Nussbaum velvet comforter. She lotions down her melanated, chocolate skin with her coconut oil and sprays her body with *A Thousand Christmas Wishes* from Bath and Body Works.

Chloe throws on a large white t-shirt and black biker shorts. She takes off her pink bonnet and sits at her vanity and begins to brush her long, black, silky hair that touches the middle of her back and puts it into a high messy bun.

Suddenly, her nose smells the aroma of baked chocolate-chip cookies, reminding her to go downstairs to take them out of the oven. Chloe then proceeds quickly to put on her pink, fuzzy slippers next to her bed. She snatches her dark pink robe off of her bedroom door, and dashes down her condo stairs to the kitchen.

The kitchen floor is made of white oak that flows into the condo's living room. Kitchen cabinets go to the ceiling to provide as much storage space as possible. Energy-efficient LED lighting under the cabinets helps give the kitchen a nice glow at night. A tall broom closet is to the right of the stainless-steel refrigerator. Beautiful countertops of marble with a satin touch. Next to the countertops is a beautiful stainless steel gas double oven with five burners, glass touch controls, self-cleaning system that removes food buildup, large oven windows that provide easy viewing of the oven's interior without opening the oven door.

Chloe quickly opens the white drawer next to the oven and puts on her, "Trust in the Lord with all your heart," oven mitt, opens the oven, and takes the cookies out and puts the cookie sheet on top of the stove. She grabs a small white plate from her tall cabinets, (standing on her tippy-toes being that she is 5"2'), and puts the small white plate on her marble countertop next to the oven. She goes to her silverware drawer and grabs an all-black spatula and puts all five cookies on her small white plate, one by one. Chloe then washes the cookie sheet and spatula with her yellow smiley face sponge with blue Dawn dish soap, bleach, and hot water, dries them with her red towel, and puts them away.

Chloe pours herself a tall glass of milk, grabs the plate of cookies, sits down on her traditional beige polyester sectional with two indigo pillows on each side, and two dark gray pillows in the middle.

The living room contains built in bookshelves and a mounted 32-inch TV cabinet in walnut. Chloe turns on a nice, chiseled natural stone fireplace. Reaches for her remote and black snuggy on her beige ottoman, turns on her television, and tries to find a great sermon to listen to and then, her iPhone 10x rings.

Chloe looks at her phone and sees it is Brandon, a man she has been dating periodically since the end of June. She hasn't heard from him in a couple of weeks. So, she rolls her eyes and doesn't answer. He calls again. Chloe picks up and says in an annoyed tone "Yes, Brandon?"

Brandon: Hey, Chloe. I know it's late, but I was thinking of you, Gorgeous.

Episode 1: Spirit Is Willing, Flesh Is Weak

Chloe: Were you really? Because I haven't heard from you. (*Taking a bite of her chocolate chip cookie.*)

Brandon: I am sorry Chloe. I have been so busy with work. There is a lot going on within my family. I meant to get back to you. What are you eating? (*Laughs.*)

Chloe: You could have told me that. And baked chocolate chip cookies.

Brandon: I know. I apologize.

Chloe: Thanks for that. So, what's up? How are you?

Brandon: I'm great. I was actually calling to see if you wanted to come over. I can cook, we can make s'mores in the backyard. Even though it seems like you are already having your dessert.

Chloe: I don't know; I'm tired and have to be up in the morning for residency. I literally just sat down to just relax.

Brandon: Come on, Chloe; just come. You can be relaxed over here. I'll make sure of it.

Chloe: Brandon, it's late. I don't... (*Interrupted by Brandon.*)

Brandon: Just come at nine. I'll be done with everything. You're only fifteen minutes away.

Chloe: You say it as if you are the one driving.

Brandon: Please, Chloe; I want to see you.

Chloe: Fine. See you in a little bit.

Brandon: Alright. See you in a minute. Bye, Gorgeous.

Chloe proceeds back upstairs to her bedroom to put on her favorite red lipstick from Cover Girl that is sitting on her vanity. She sits down, looking into her vanity mirror, puts the red lipstick on her top lip from left to right and does the same to the bottom, thinking to herself, "I should just tell him I am not coming. I have not heard from him. I should not just jump when he says jump."

She stands up and goes into her closet to grab her favorite brand 'You're Worth More' black hoodie, shirt, and fitted sweats. Puts on her white Nike Air Max 97 shoes on the side of her bed. Says to herself, "I'm just going to go.

I'm dressed now anyway." Chloe looks at the clock on her vanity and notices it's 8:45 pm. Chloe hurries and snatches her red Guess purse off her bedroom door, and grabs her keys off her dresser.

As she is rushing downstairs, her roommate, Mya, comes through the door and asks, "Where are you going in a hurry, Miss Thang?" Chloe replies nervously, "To Brandon's." Mya then says "Oh gosh! Didn't he blow you off for a couple of weeks?" Chloe puts her hand on the knob of the door, trying to leave, and laughs and says, "We will talk about it later, girl." Mya laughs, "Alrighty, be safe."

Chloe jumps into her black 2013 Toyota Camry and plays old-school gospel music by one of her favorite gospel artist. Thinking to herself, "Should I even really be going to his house? Mya is right. He did blow me off for a couple weeks. However, he has been going through some things."

Chloe finally arrives at Brandon's one-story glass home. She parks on the opposite side of the street because his garbage cans are put out to be ready to be dumped tomorrow morning. Chloe pulls down her visor to check how her lipstick looks and says, "Man, I should just go home. However, Brandon is a great guy who works hard in his field of architecture and has been working for himself for about five years. So, I can give him the benefit of the doubt. Right? Life just happens and his business is fairly new. He is a successful Black man in his late twenties. However, his cautiousness on who he lets in is frustrating. I understand that different women have used him for his money, but it isn't right to put those trust issues on me. I have my own money. Brandon is a true gentleman, opening doors, wining and dining, great active listener, and has respect for me. The man is fine too! With his flawless caramel skin, beautiful pearly white smile, dark brown eyes, hair full of waves, and a nice clean goatee, broad shoulders, muscular arms, 5 foot 11, just like I like them. Most importantly, he was raised in the church like me. My only issue is that he doesn't trust the church anymore because of the things that he has seen and experienced. I'm not discrediting what he went through, but I want him to understand God isn't the one who did it. God gives people free will. Brandon did tell me I can help him open up to attending again. He didn't say he did not love God; he just needs time to trust in God again. I'm here anyway."

Chloe then closes her visor. She looks to the left and sees Brandon opening up his front door and he begins waving at Chloe. He motions with his arm for her to just park in his driveway, so she does. He opens Chloe's car door when she parks in his driveway and says, "You look cute with your little messy bun." He squeezes her tight and says in a mocking voice, "I missed you, little shortie," and begins to laugh (being that Chloe is 28 years old and 5"2' tall). As he squeezes her tightly, Chloe falls into his muscular abs and smells his Cool Water cologne and wishes to just stay in that position forever. He tells her, "Come on, let's go inside; it's cold out here. Make sure to lock your doors."

Chloe enters Brandon's luxurious, fully furnished, four-bedroom home, full of cream, grey, and hints of yellow colors. Beautiful canvases on his walls, and family photos placed so elegantly. The living room is spacious with three large rectangular, wide glass windows covered with extra-long curtains, two-story drapes, and white linen. A beautiful corner sectional couch with two yellow pillows in the corner and one cream pillow in the middle about two feet away from the windows. Facing Brandon's entertainment center is a nice sleek white 135-inch TV. His home is organized so well. You would think you were at a library.

Chloe smells an aroma of BBQ baked chicken, green beans, and Spanish rice. Brandon directs Chloe to his falling extendable white dining room table. When the table is fully extended the capacity is ten people. Because it was just himself and Chloe, he fully collapsed the table, which occupied six people.

When Chloe approaches the table, she sees unaccented gold taper candles lit, a glass of Cabernet red wine, and a plate prepared for her. Chloe's eyes are in disbelief. Chloe smiles at Brandon, showing her white, immaculately straight teeth. He smiles back and says, "Didn't know I could get down like this, did you?" Chloe then states, "I mean how could I when you ghost me for a couple of weeks?" Brandon pulls out the upholstered white chair, curved padded seat with backrest, stainless steel cabriole legs, located in front of Chloe's plate at the head of the table.

When Chloe sits down, Brandon helps by pushing her chair closer to the table. Brandon then says, "You aren't going to let those few weeks go are you?" Chloe then says to Brandon, "Nope! Own it sir. But you fancy huh?" Brandon begins doing an old-school dance called the Douggie, on his way to his chair right across from Chloe, and sings the 'Fancy' song by changing up the words. "Table done, food done, everything done. Oh you fancy huh?" says Brandon. They both laugh and reminisce on how old the song is. They begin to eat, and Brandon is staring at Chloe, hoping she is enjoying her food. Chloe gives Brandon some relief by looking into his dark brown eyes with a smile, stating, "I'm not going to lie to you, Brandon; this is actually really good." Brandon smiles and takes a sip of his Cabernet wine and states, "I'm delighted that you enjoyed it. I wanted to do something special for you. I apologize for not speaking with you for weeks. That wasn't okay. You are right. I could have told you what was going on. I just haven't had a real woman that actually cared." Chloe looks straight into Brandon's eyes with a stern look and says, "Be consistent with me and you'll be used to it." Brandon smiles, "Okay, I can do that."

As he is getting up from his chair he grabs his completed dinner plate then grabs Chloe's while asking, "Are you ready for dessert? I promised you s'mores. It is a beautiful night too. Besides the coldness." Chloe gets up and follows Brandon into the kitchen, saying excitedly, "Yes, I am! Do you want my help with washing dishes?" Brandon responds quickly "Absolutely not. You're here to relax. You can go ahead and grab your wine glass off the table, and I'll meet you outside. I got this, future doctor. Do you remember how to turn on the heaters?" he asks jokingly. Chloe chuckles, "Yes, I remember, Brandon." "Glad to hear you do! You may be wifey one day. Grab those two throw covers on my ottoman so you won't be cold. I'll be out there in a minute." Chloe then grabs her wine glass, two throw covers while smiling, saying, "Meet you outside."

She slides the tall sliding glass backyard door open. She puts her wine glass on the fire pit and wraps herself up with one of the grey throw covers. Then turns on the heaters next to Brandon's Highland Point fire pit seating set. It is highlighted by a seamless fusion of modern aesthetics with a traditional flair. Chloe sits on one of the high-quality aluminum chair frames that includes seat cushions made of premium polyester fiber batting wrapped around a high resiliency foam core. Chloe turns on the Smart TV on the wall and plays some old 90's music on YouTube while Brandon is getting everything ready. Chloe looks through the tall glass sliding door and sees Brandon aiming to make everything perfect. Chloe thinks to herself, "This could work. Brandon and me. I just need him to be consistent. This is great but is he just doing it for right now? I'm two years away from thirty. I do not want to play games anymore."

Brandon begins coming towards the door, smiling at her and she smirks at him right back. Chloe opens the sliding door for Brandon while he's holding a tray of marshmallows, cinnamon Graham crackers, Hershey's chocolate bars, napkins, and a bottle of Cabernet wine. He sets the tray in the middle of the two of them. While saying...

Brandon: You got it warm out here, girl. Are you ready for s'mores and wine?

Chloe: Always. Thank you. So, what are your intentions with me, Brandon?

Brandon: (*Looks at Chloe and smiles as he is putting marshmallows on his stick as well as on Chloe's.*) Just straight to the point huh? Well, I want to intentionally date you. I can see myself marrying you one day. (*Hands Chloe her stick of marshmallows.*)

Chloe: (*Puts her stick of marshmallows into the fire pit.*) How are you sure you are ready to date though? Or ready to be with someone for that matter?

Brandon: (*Standing up, putting his s'more together.*) I'm getting older. I will be thirty in the next year, and I don't want to play games. I want to share this house with someone and build an empire with them.

Chloe: (*Smiles.*) Okay, I believe you. However, I need to see action now. We have been talking for six months now on and off. I have to protect myself. (*Bites her s'more and sips her wine in amazement.*) This s'more is bomb, especially with this wine!

Brandon: I know, Chloe; you're right. I will show you I am serious. (*Sweet Lady by Tyrese comes on.*) Let's dance.

Chloe: Really ? Right now?

Brandon pulls Chloe up. Pulls her in close with his muscular arms and whispers in her ear, "I almost lost you and I don't plan to do that again. I honestly want to only date you and you only date me. Is that okay?" Chloe looks at him uncertainly. He smiles at her and tells her, "You can trust me. I just want you." Chloe smiles and says, "Okay, but I have to see that through your actions." Brandon pulls her in closer and says, "You're so beautiful. He pulls her chin up and kisses her on her lips. Chloe begins to think, "I should probably leave right now before I end up compromising myself again with him." Chloe pulls away from Brandon.

Chloe: I should go, Brandon.

Brandon: Why? What's wrong?

Chloe: It is late, I have to wake up early tomorrow. It is almost eleven. I need to think about all this.

Episode 1: Spirit Is Willing, Flesh Is Weak

Brandon: Okay, I understand. I am serious about you, Chloe.

Chloe: Okay, we will see.

Chloe then opens the sliding door, goes to the front door, and grabs her purse off the rack next to the door. Before she opens the door, Brandon pulls Chloe's waist in for a passionate kiss. Chloe is standing on her tiptoes, holding his neck. Brandon begins moving Chloe towards the couch and lays her down. He takes off his shirt and is laying on top of her, continuing to kiss Chloe passionately.

Brandon: (*Gets up.*) Are you ready for this? I know you're waiting.

Chloe: Yes, I'm good. (*She speaks nervously and unsure.*)

Brandon: Okay, just wait. I'll be right back.

Chloe: What am I doing? I am almost thirty though. I am not trying to be a thirty-five or forty-year-old virgin. I mean, other people who have had sex unmarried are perfectly fine. They even end up marrying the person. Why can't I do the same? Man, I don't know. Brandon said just wait; he will be right back. So, I'll just wait.

Chloe: How did I get here? (*Chloe begins thinking back to how she and Brandon even met. Her heart is pounding, and she is extremely nervous.*)

Episode 2: IN THE BEGINNING

It is the beginning of summer on a Monday morning in mid-June 2015. Chloe is laying on her queen-size bed with a Nussbaum velvet comforter, her hair wrapped underneath her silk pink bonnet, with her Tommy Hilfiger pajamas two-piece set she found on sale at Ross. Wakes up to her alarm going off at 5:00 am to arrive at her residency by 7:00. She gets up, happy that she took a shower the night before. She plays "Respond" by Travis Green on her JBL Flip 5 speaker. Makes her queen-size bed back up, making sure everything is straight in their corners and each pillow is put back on her bed properly.

Chloe then goes into her closet to take out her lab coat, which is required, along with her identifiable name badges (MSM and Hospital ID) to be worn while within the hospital. She takes out her nice short-sleeve blouse and knee-length black skirt. Grabs her red closed toe Calvin Klein heels she also found at Ross on sale, and her white tennis shoes. Chloe lays the clothes she will be wearing on the bed and places her shoes by her door where her medical bag is.

She goes into the bathroom, brushes her teeth with her electronic Colgate toothbrush around in a circular motion, with Colgate toothpaste, of course. After rinsing her mouth, she begins flossing her teeth. Looks in the mirror and smiles, then grabs her Shea Moisture Scrub to wash her face, rinses with warm water, then pats her face with a dry face towel, and lotions her face with Shea Moisture Lotion. She then takes off her pink bonnet, puts it into her drawer, and grabs her red hairbrush and brushes her silky black hair back to put into a high ponytail and puts edge control on her edges.

Chloe steps outside of her bathroom, grabs her red short-sleeve ruffled blouse off the bed, and puts it on. Picks up her black knee-high length skirt, putting it on but wiggling it up to get it passed her thighs. She then stuffs part of her red blouse down her skirt and zips the back of her skirt up from behind. She looks into her mirror and says to herself, "Man, my shape is looking good." She goes to her vanity and sits down, and looking into her vanity mirror, puts on a nude lip gloss on her top lip from left to right and does the same to the bottom. She looks into the mirror and says, "You are beautiful; God loves you; today will be a great day because of how much God loves you. Oh, my watch! I need to put it on." She puts on the Coach watch her father gave her. Looks at the time, which is 5:45 am and says, "I have enough time to try this new devotional book." She goes to her nightstand, opens her drawer, and takes out

Episode 2: In the Beginning

her devotional book, *Blossoming Nicely*, written by Areva Denise Neely.

Protea (Transformation)

"Show up in every moment like you're meant to be there," said Marie Forleo. This will be a week of transforming, courage, and diversity, which the protea flower symbolizes. Transform means to make a thorough, or dramatic change in the form, appearance, or character of. Joshua 24:15 says, *"And if it is evil in your eyes to serve the LORD, choose this day whom you will serve, whether the gods your fathers served in the region beyond the River, or the gods of the Amorites in whose land you dwell. But as for me and my house, we will serve the LORD."* Once we determine that we're going to serve God, the transformation will come with having intimate time with God. Romans 12:2 says, *"Do not be conformed to this world, but be transformed by the renewal of your mind, that by testing you may discern what is the will of God, what is good and acceptable and perfect."*

Seed - 1

Protea (Transformation)

As Nancy Pearcy said in her phenomenal book, *Finding Truth*, "I studied my way back to God." If we're sincerely looking for a transformation in our hearts, we have to ask ourselves questions about why we believe what we believe. What are we doing to help others? Are we a dismissive or defensive Christian? Do we have a defense for what we believe? These are sometimes scary questions. But as Timothy Keller said, "Doubt your doubts."

Transformation can sometimes feel uncomfortable but if we are always comfortable, how can we truly transform? James 1:2-3 tells us to *"Count it all joy, my brothers, when you meet trials of various kinds, for you know that the testing of your faith produces steadfastness."* For instance, a woman has to go through a transformational change within her body in order to deliver her baby. The process of the transformation is uncomfortable and can become extremely painful. Sometimes unbearable. However, this has to happen to bring forth a beautiful daughter or son from the Lord. In the end, the transformation was worth seeing a beautiful healthy child.

Romans 8:18 says, *"I consider that our present sufferings are not worth comparing with the glory that will be revealed in us.*" This is why it is also key to understand that just because we believe in God does not mean we will not go through trials or trouble. That's the Christian life.

Seed - 2

Blossoming Nicely

Paul said in Romans 5:3-4, "*Not only that, but we rejoice in our sufferings, knowing that suffering produces endurance, and endurance produces character, and character produces hope.*" Yet, we are able to go to God's Word for help and comfort. 1 Corinthians 1:3-4 says, "*Blessed be the God and Father of our Lord Jesus Christ, the Father of mercies and God of all comfort, who comforts us in all our affliction, so that we may be able to comfort those who are in any affliction, with the comfort with which we ourselves are comforted by God.*" He's Abba, our Father. Just as when a child falls off a bicycle, a natural father runs to help his son or daughter up, and hugs and comforts them, our heavenly Father surely does the same for us. We just have to acknowledge Him and believe.

Matthew 6:26 tells us to "*Look at the birds of the air: they neither sow nor reap nor gather into barns, and yet your heavenly Father feeds them. Are you not of more value than they?*" He cares for us more than we could ever begin to imagine. *"But, as it is written, 'What no eye has seen, nor ear heard, nor the heart of man imagined, what God has prepared for those who love him'"* 1 Corinthians 2:9

Seed - 3

Protea (Transformation)

We must lean on Him to transform us to His purpose. He has chosen us way before the foundation of the world to be His. Proverbs 3:5-6 says, *"Trust in the Lord with all your heart, and do not lean on your own understanding. In all your ways acknowledge him, and he will make straight paths."* Jeremiah 1:5 tells us, *"Before I formed you in the womb I knew you, and before you were born I consecrated you; I appointed you a prophet to the nations."*

We have to be courageous enough to have a diverse way of thinking, more like Christ. This comes with understanding you are a new creation, as we are told in 2 Corinthians 5:17, *"Therefore, if anyone is in Christ, he is a new creation. The old has passed away, behold, the new has come."* So, during your bloom time for the week, go purchase or grow a protea. Meditate on seeing yourself as a new creation in Christ. Ask yourself what that really means. How is your personal relationship with God and what do you want to see more of with Him? Don't worry. I'll be giving you a breakdown of how to do this after every chapter. Take your time. Do not rush. Become intimate with the Father, grow a stronger bond with Jesus, and be sensitive to the Holy Spirit. Matthew 11:15 admonishes us, *"He who has ears to hear, let him hear."*

As Chloe ends her time of devotion, she asks herself the question, "How have I been transformed? What does it mean to be a new creation through Jesus Christ?" She makes a mental note to make sure to write out what the scriptures spoke to her during this time and then write out a prayer in the Notes section at the end of this particular chapter in her devotional, so that she can look back and see what God has done in her life.

Meditate on Romans 12:2-3 and 2 Corinthians 5:17-21.

It is now 6:15 am and Chloe realizes, "Ok, I got to get moving." She grabs her medical bag, purse, and her keys by the door. Chloe's roommate, Mya, who is always up early making breakfast, is a 9th grade English teacher. She always says to Chloe, "Good morning, Chloe girl. Let's go get our money." Chloe says, "Good morning, girlie; let's go get it." She grabs a banana and her lunch pail of baked chicken, packaged Caesar salad, grapes, and pink water bottle, then rushes towards the door, grabs all of her belongings, and rushes out the door. Chloe gets into her car by 6:20 am. Conveniently for her, the hospital is 15 minutes away. She arrives at 6:40 am because of traffic. When she arrives at the hospital she goes straight to her locker and puts everything away. She places her lunch in the refrigerator and changes into her blue scrubs with her white doctoral coat. Her co-resident, Joshua, who is 5'9", fit, curly hair, with a nice clean fade and beard, Dominican and Puerto Rican, sees her walking out the locker room and says to Chloe:

Joshua: Are you ready for this conference this morning to go over senior morning reports, Grand Rounds, and these boring faculty presentations? So glad we don't have to do a presentation today.

Chloe: Josh, you know I stay ready. Don't think of the presentations as boring but insightful, plus we're learning something new to make us great doctors.

Joshua: (*Laughs.*) Chloe, now you know these presentations are boring. Stop kissing up.

Episode 2: In the Beginning

Chloe: No one is kissing up. I'm just saying if we have to sit and listen to these presentations, we might as well see something positive out of it.

Joshua: I guess, Chloe. So, when are you going to let me take you on a date?

Chloe: When you learn how to communicate better. See you in the conference room, Joshua. (*Chloe walks away.*)

Joshua: (*Smirks as Chloe walks away.*) You will say yes eventually. See you there, beautiful.

Chloe arrives in the conference room after receiving sign-outs from the team the night before, to check out all the vital signs of different outcomes of the patients overnight. The conference room allows a maximum of 25 people. Chloe has five residents in her group, including herself. Chloe has always been about being early her whole life. Being early gives you more opportunity to plan, speak, think, and pray. So of course, Chloe was the first to arrive in the conference room. Her attending, Dr. O'Leary, walks in the room. He's 6'4", handsome, ocean waves in his hair, mustache clean cut, Caucasian and Black, with beautiful hazel eyes honey skin.

Dr. O'Leary: Good morning, Chloe, how is our patient, Marisa, doing today?

Chloe: (*Confidently*) She is doing great. Since her tonsils were removed, her airway for breathing has been much better.

Joshua: (*Walks in.*) Actually, it says in her chart she had difficulty breathing afterwards and we have to be sure to check on her consistently today.

Dr. O'Leary: Thanks for that, Joshua. Chloe, getting here early does not mean anything if you are not paying close attention to the paperwork. Great doctors look at the smallest details.

Joshua: (*Smirks at Chloe.*)

Chloe: Yes, sir. I apologize. (*Nicholas and Patrice, who are residents, walk in.*)

Dr. O'Leary: Apologies aren't for me. This is for all of you to know. And Josh, I saw that smirk on your face. You were late a couple of times last week and didn't do great jobs with putting in IVs. You're a 3rd year? Come on, do better. As doctors, it is our job to pay close attention to our patients' charts. We can't give them constant apologies when dealing with things we can control. We are here to save lives! So, let's get to work. Check all your charts and get moving. Chloe, come speak to me, please.

Dr. O'Leary (*outside the door in hallway*): Let's do lunch after the noon lecture. We need to talk.

Chloe: Is everything okay? What did I do?

Dr. O'Leary: Nothing, Chloe. We just need to talk. Meet me at Hole in the Wall Cafe around the corner at 1:45 pm. The lecture will be from 12-1:30 pm I know your lunch is at 2 pm. I'll be sure we're back by 2:30 pm. I'll have someone cover you. Okay?

Chloe: Okay.

Dr. O'Leary: And stay focused. Don't let Joshua get under your skin. See you later, chaser. Get to work.

(*Chloe goes back into the conference room.*)

Joshua: Chloe, how does it feel to finally be beat by me?

Patricia (*Beautiful, 5'9", natural curly hair, slim, dark brown eyes, raspy voice, Black and Hispanic*): I should've known you had something to do with him giving us that lecture.

Joshua: Hey don't blame me. I paid attention to the patient's chart. It's Little Miss Perfect Chloe Chaser over here who didn't.

Chloe: Ugh! Bite me, Josh.

Joshua: Would love to! (*Smiling hard.*)

Chloe: Like you would ever have the chance!

Nicholas (*Black, 6'0", handsome, light skin, curly hair, fit, beautiful white smile, and southern voice*): Come on, you two. We do not have time for this! Josh, stop. We're a team, y'all. Let's look at our other charts. Especially before the lecture this afternoon.

As Chloe and her team are going room to room checking on their patients, she is thinking to herself, "What possibly does Dr. O'Leary want to talk to me about?" Chloe thought to herself, "I have been doing well with everything besides this morning. That was a big dumb mistake I can't believe I missed."

Patrice: (*Walking out of the patient room with her group.*) Man, you guys, I cannot believe we're almost done!

Joshua: I know. I'm not trying to go to this lecture today, though.

Nicholas: Get over it. Be happy we're even here, man.

Patrice: Right! I dreamed of this for so long. How are you feeling, Chloe?

Chloe: (*Thinking of what Dr. O'Leary wants to talk about.*)

Patrice: Chloe?

Chloe: Oh sorry! I'm excited too.

Patrice: What's going on?

Joshua: She's nervous because I one-upped her today. (*Laughs.*)

Chloe: (*Rolls her eyes and chuckles.*)

Nicholas: (*Shakes his head and laughs.*) Josh, come with me. Let's go get a snack. We will meet you ladies at the lecture hall.

Patrice: (*Stops her and sits down on a bench in the hallway in the hospital.*) What's going on? I saw Dr. O'Leary pull you to the side. Is everything okay?

Chloe: Don't worry about it, Patrice. I'll be okay.

Patrice: Your joy and faith usually always uplifts me. So, are you sure?

Chloe: Yes, come on. I want to get to the lecture early.

Patrice: (*Laughs.*) Of course you do. Okay, but I'm going to have those two knuckleheads bring us snacks, too. (*Laughs.*)

Episode 2: In the Beginning

All residents, including Chloe walk out of the lecture. Chloe's team offers to have lunch with her in the cafeteria. Chloe kindly declines and tells them she already had plans to meet someone for lunch.

Joshua: Well, it's not with me, so who is it?

Chloe: Bye Josh.

Chloe proceeds to her locker and grabs her purse and lunch out of the refrigerator. When she arrives at the Cafe she walks in and sees Dr. O'Leary sitting down in the back. Her heart begins to beat fast. Dr. O'Leary gets up and pulls out her chair and kisses her cheek. Chloe smiles.

Dr. O'Leary: I know we both don't have that much time. We have to get back to the hospital. I want to make sure we eat but also have this conversation.

Waitress: What would you like to drink to start off?

Dr. O'Leary: I would like sparkling water, please.

Chloe: I will have a coffee with extra cream, please.

Waitress: Are you ready to order?

Dr. O'Leary: Actually yes. I would like to have the chicken salad, please.

Chloe: I'm okay. Thank you. I'm going to eat the lunch I have.

Waitress: Got it.

Chloe: So, what do you need to tell me?

Dr. O'Leary: Look Chloe, (*Grabs her hands and holds it on top of the table beside a small vase with a small rose inside.*) I really like you. I've enjoyed spending time with you and getting to know you outside the hospital. But I've been dating you for a year and with you officially for two months and we still haven't had sex.

Chloe: (*Pulls her hands away and puts them underneath the table.*) Ethan, I can't.

Dr. O'Leary: Why can't you?

Episode 2: In the Beginning

Chloe: I'm still a virgin and I'm waiting to save myself until marriage.

Dr. O'Leary: (*Silent.*)

Chloe: Say something.

Waitress: (*Brings sparkling water and coffee.*) Here you go, sir, your sparkling water; and here you go, beautiful, your coffee with extra cream.

Chloe and Dr. O'Leary: Thank you.

Waitress: No, problem. Be out with your food soon, sir.

Chloe: (*Looks at Ethan with a regretful face while taking her food out of her lunch pail.*) Are you going to say something?

Dr. O'Leary (*speaking in a calm frustrated tone*): You don't think this is something you should have told me when we first began talking? Even before we made it official two months ago. To give me the choice of even wanting to wait?

Chloe: I told you I was a virgin.

Dr. O'Leary: That doesn't mean I knew you wanted to wait until you were married.

Chloe: I apologize. I should've told you. I shouldn't have assumed you knew that.

Dr. O'Leary: Chloe, I know you did not mean harm but baby I can't do it. I do see you as my wife one day but no time soon.

Chloe: So, what are you saying? (*Eyes watery as she looks down at her food.*)

Dr. O'Leary: It's up to you. I like you and I care about you deeply, but I don't want to wait that long. Do you plan to have sex with me in the next month or two?

Chloe: No, I don't. (*Looking down.*)

Dr. O'Leary: Then I can't be with you. I'm sorry. If you would've told me sooner then we wouldn't be here right now. Let's just eat and go back to work. Then we can talk when we get off. I respect you for standing for what you believe in but it's not what I signed up for. I'm sorry.

Episode 2: In the Beginning

Chloe: (*Gets up and speaks in a shaky voice.*) I'm going to go to the restroom. I'll be right back.

The waitress passes by Chloe with Dr. O'Leary's food.

Chloe: (*Walks in the bathroom. Goes into a bathroom stall and cries. Begins to talk to herself in frustration.*) Why didn't I tell him? I should've told him when we first met. But when I do that sometimes they say it's fine and then leave, or say it isn't going to work months later. I'm tired of this! My heart is so broken. I don't even want to sit and eat with him. Maybe I should stop waiting? I can't do this anymore! God help me get through this. I know what you're telling me to do is not in vain. (*Crying uncontrollably.*)

Waitress (*Walks in and touches the outside of the bathroom stall*): Excuse me ma'am? Are you alright?

Chloe: (*Gets herself together and walks out of the stall.*)

Waitress: Hey sweetie. (*Hand on her shoulder.*) What's going on?

Chloe: Oh, it's nothing. I'll be okay.

Waitress: Well, let me tell you this. I know you don't know me. However, when I came to your table I saw God's light just shining down on you. You are such a beautiful soul, and it was a joy to serve you. Know this! Whatever you're going through, God always has a way of turning it around and giving you something greater. Just trust in Him even when you feel as if it's not worth it. Everything He has us wait for is always worth the wait.

Chloe: (*Cries and hugs her.*)

Waitress: Now go enjoy your lunch. And let me use this restroom, wash my hands, and go on my break. God bless you, my darling.

Chloe: You too.

Chloe sits down back at her table and eats a little bit of her lunch.

Dr. O'Leary: Hey we have to get back to the hospital. We have about 15 minutes. I already paid.

Episode 2: In the Beginning

Chloe: Yeah, you're right.

Dr. O'Leary: Are you okay?

Chloe: (*Thinks in her head, "What do you think?" Instead, she speaks in a calm voice.*) I will be. Let's go. (*Puts the remainder of her lunch in her lunch pail.*)

Dr. O'Leary and Chloe walk out of the cafe towards their cars. Then Chloe realizes she doesn't have her purse. Chloe insists that Dr. O'Leary meet her back at the hospital. Dr. O'Leary hugs her and kisses her on her forehead and says, "Okay, see you there." Chloe rushes back into the cafe to the register and bumps into a flawless caramel skin, beautiful pearly white smile, dark brown eyes, hair full of waves, a nice clean goatee, broad shoulders, muscular arms, 5'11", navy blue clean suit wearing man.

Chloe: Oh my gosh! I am so sorry! I got your coffee all over you! I'll buy you another one as soon as I find my purse. I really apologize. What's your name ?

Brandon: It is okay. My name is Brandon, and I am happy I bumped into you because I just turned your purse in. I see you left kind of flustered.

Chloe: Oh wow. Thank you so much. Let me get you another coffee. It's the least I can do.

Brandon: How about your number ? If you're single?

Chloe: (*Laughs.*) Coffee or nothing?

Brandon: If not your number what about your Instagram? And a coffee? I know you have one?

Chloe: One or the other, sir? (*Laughs.*)

Brandon: I'll take the Instagram. (*Brandon hands Chloe his phone.*)

Chloe: See you around, Brandon. Thank you again. (*Rushing out of the café.*)

Brandon: No problem. (*Looking at his phone on Instagram and whispering to himself, "@Chloeissuccesful"*

Chloe arrives back at the hospital at 2:30 pm, which for Chloe means she's late. She rushes in to the hospital, goes to her locker to put her things away, and washes her

41

hands. She checks in and goes on her rounds. As time passes, it's almost 5:00 in the evening. She fills out all the necessary paperwork in the conference room, making sure everything is in order for the next residents who come in.

Joshua: Hey, Chloe. What a day, right?

Chloe: What do you want, Josh?

Joshua: (*Laughs.*) I'm just trying to have a conversation with you.

Chloe: I know you want something.

Joshua: Yes, for you to go get a drink and dinner with me tonight.

Chloe: (*Laughs.*) Josh, no. For one we have to be back here early in the morning and I'm tired. And sorry; I wouldn't date you.

Joshua: Okay. (*Patrice and Nicholas walk in.*) How about we all go eat and get drinks together.

Patrice: I'm okay with it.

Nicholas: Me too.

Joshua: See? Not a date. Chloe, come on.

Chloe: Fine. Where are we going ?

Joshua: There is a nice five-star rating Mexican restaurant 15 minutes away from here that has amazing food and drinks. Who is down for Mexican?

Patrice and Chloe look at one another and shake their heads yes nonchalantly as they grab all their belongings.

Nicholas: Alright let's go.

Castaneda's Mexican Food is a Mexican rustic restaurant that has elements that include wood or wood-like materials, polished, acid-washed concrete floors, and the natural look of wood on walls and tables. Castaneda's has a real authentic look like where you would find food in a Mexican village. The murals and Mexican flag colors also help bring an urban feel that creates an authentic Mexican look. Their food is known to be vibrant, delicious, and fresh.

As Chloe and her co-residents walk into the restaurant, they can smell the fresh aroma of tortillas, chilies being scorched on a direct flame, tacos getting ready to be made with the spicy, and marinated meat offset by the sweet pineapple. The waitress recognizes Josh.

Waitress: Hola, Josh. I see you invited some of your amigos.

Joshua: Yes, senorita; I did.

Patrice, Nicholas, and Chloe look at one another, laughing and shaking their heads.

Joshua: Don't mind my haters.

Waitress: I have a great table for you right next to the stage. There will be a performance tonight.

Patrice: Awesome! Thank you so much.

Waitress: Follow me.

Joshua: See, with me you get V.I.P.

Chloe: Oh shut up, Josh. (*While laughing and getting ready to sit down next to Patrice.*)

Joshua: You're sitting next to me tonight. (*He scoots over in the booth.*)

Chloe: Alright. I'll give you that wish.

Nicholas and Patrice begin laughing and sit across from the both of them on the other side of the booth.

Waitress: Here are your menus. Would you all like to start off with something to drink? I know Josh would like our classic margarita.

Joshua: Yes, and they will too. First round is on me.

Nicholas: Sounds good to me. Thanks bro.

Waitress: Alright. I'll be right back with your drinks and chips and salsa. I'll give you time to look at our menu.

Joshua: It's a cool little spot, right?

Episode 2: In the Beginning

Patrice and Chloe both respond by saying yes.

Nicholas: Yes, I like it. What do you usually get from here?

Joshua: I enjoy their chicken fajitas. Make sure you get their special house salsa on the side.

Nicholas: Okay, I'm going to go ahead and get that too.

Patrice: Me as well.

Chloe: I don't think I trust Josh. I'm going to get something else. (*Laughs.*) No, I'm playing. I'm going to try it too.

Joshua: Yeah, you better.

Waitress: Here are your classic margaritas and chips and salsa. Do you all know what you're ordering this evening or need more time?

Joshua: We're going to have your chicken fajitas with the special house salsa on the side.

Waitress: Sounds good. I'll get that in for you. Do you all want another round of drinks?

Nicholas: I'll buy the next round.

Chloe: Then I am done after that.

Waitress: Alright I'll get that in for you all right away.

Performer comes on stage, and she is dressed in a beautiful garment and begins to sing "Como La Flor" by Selena. Patrice and Chloe begin singing with her, laughing. Nicholas and Josh look at them just laughing.

Patrice: You want to dance, Nick?

Nicholas: You got to teach me a little something. I'm not great. (*Begins laughing.*)

Patrice: Great! Makes it more fun.

Patrice grabs Nicholas' hand and they begin salsa dancing on the dance floor. Well, we can see that Nicholas is learning.

Episode 2: In the Beginning

Joshua: You want to dance ?

Chloe: Sure, why not?

Josh grabs Chloe's hand and they're just having a great time. Patrice says, "Come on, guys; switch partners." Patrice begins dancing with Josh. Nicholas is learning with Chloe. Until Brandon, whom Chloe met at the café, taps her on her shoulder.

Brandon: Hey, don't I know you from somewhere? Like somewhere this afternoon? Do you look familiar? (*Asking jokingly.*)

Chloe: (*Looks him up and down.*) Maybe?

Josh, Patrice, and Nicholas stop dancing as they're trying to figure out who this person is.
The waitress brings their food to the table.

Joshua: Hey you guys, she brought our food to the table.

Chloe: Okay. I'll be over there in a minute.

Brandon: So, we meet again?

Chloe: I guess we do.

Brandon: So, I know none of those men are your boyfriends because they wouldn't dare leave you over here with me?

Chloe: Correct. Those are coworkers. But we've been through a lot with one another in this residency program.

Brandon: Oh, so you're a doctor or nurse?

Chloe: Doctor. Thank you.

Brandon: Okay, Ms. Doctor. Do you mind if I take you out this weekend?

Chloe: I literally just got out of a relationship. That is not a good idea.

Brandon: I saw you twice in one day. What are the odds?

Chloe: Try a third time. Gotta go; my food is getting cold.

Episode 2: In the Beginning

Brandon: (*Smirks.*)

Chloe: Sorry about that, you guys.

Joshua: So, who is that?

Chloe: Just someone I ran into earlier.

Patrice: Oh my gosh, Josh; these fajitas are good. And Chloe, you're not fooling me. You have a glow on your face.

Brandon: (*Walks over to the table.*) Sorry to interrupt.

Joshua: Then don't.

Nicholas: Josh, eat your food.

Chloe: Sorry; excuse him.

Brandon: (*Laughs.*) It's okay. I know you said you just got out of a relationship.

Patrice: Oh really?

Chloe: It's complicated.

Patrice: Yeah. We will talk.

Brandon: (*Laughs.*) But you're just such a beauty. I can tell you have a big heart and I just want to get to know you. Even just as a friend, what do you say?

Patrice: Yes.

Chloe: Patrice!

Patrice: Chloe!

Chloe: Fine. But as a friend.

Joshua: Yeah. A buddy friend.

Brandon: Well, can I have your number now?

Chloe: You remember, you have my Instagram.

Brandon: (*Laughs.*) Fair. (*While holding his to-go bag.*) I'll speak with you later.

Chloe: (*Smiles.*) Okay, later.

Episode 2: In the Beginning

Patrice: We have so much to talk about.

Nicholas: Let her live.

Joshua: I agree with Patrice.

Chloe: Thank you, Nicholas. (*Laughs.*) Josh, eat your food.

They all begin eating, laughing, and talking about relationships, and work. Chloe is the first to call it a night, ready to pay for her check. The waitress brings her the check and gives her a container seeing that she didn't finish all her food. She hugs Josh when she gets up. Tells everyone goodnight and that she will see them in the morning. As she is walking towards her car, her phone rings.

Chloe: (*Nervously*) Hi, Ethan.

Dr. O'Leary: Hey, I know it is late. How are you doing?

Chloe: I'm fine.

Dr. O'Leary: I apologize how everything went earlier.

Chloe: It's fine. Just time for us to move on. You don't want to wait, and I have to be okay with that.

Dr. O'Leary: I really care for you deeply and I know you do for me. We both know we are going to get married to one another one day. So, what is the big deal?

Chloe: (Chloe takes a deep breath) Well if we both know that then we can wait. We will have all of our life together to have sex. But you know what? That statement right there, no offense to you, just means you are not the one for me and I am not the one for you. Does it hurt? Yes, but it would hurt even more if I compromised myself to make you happy or just to make this relationship work.

Dr. O'Leary: You know what? You're right. I wish things could have gone differently. You are a beautiful woman and I know one day you'll receive the man you have been praying for. I wish you the best, Chloe. Don't worry either. Work will be work and I'll be your attendant and still treat you with the respect you deserve. You know I'm about professionalism.

Chloe: I know.

Episode 2: In the Beginning

Dr. O'Leary: I do want you to know I really care for you deeply, Chloe. But I understand. Take care and see you in the morning. Have a good night.

Chloe: See you in the morning. Goodnight.

Episode 3: COURTSHIP

Three months have passed, and Chloe finally says yes to Brandon to go on a date after having a few phone conversations and coffee meetups. Brandon decides to take Chloe to the San Diego Zoo. Chloe is hesitant because for one, she does not care for the zoo. Secondly, she thinks that it may be too early for her to begin dating again. However, she knows she cannot just sit in the house hoping that someone will find her there. So, she decides to give it a shot. Why not?

Brandon informs Chloe that he will be picking her up at 10:30 am Saturday morning to take her to their reservation for brunch at 11:00 am, located at The Corner Drafthouse, located in Bankers Hill, San Diego, featuring daily happy hour specials. Co-owners David C. and Dan S. curated the craft beer-centric concept, which is a must-try for brunch, lunch, and dinner. Regulars also enjoy the Mug Club and other daily and monthly promotions. The neighborhood gastropub is located one block from Balboa Park and 1.8 miles from the San Diego International Airport. It is a cozy local hangout with a wraparound patio, serving gastropub fare and southern California brews. Then after, they will head to the San Diego Zoo.

Episode 3: Courtship

Saturday morning, Chloe's alarm goes off at 8 am. Chloe gets out of bed, grabs her dark pink robe off the back of her bedroom door, and throws it over the shower. She turns on the shower as hot as she can get it. Turns on one of her favorite songs, "Wait It Out," by Jamie Grace, and hops into the shower while singing along.

Chloe's phone begins to go off with text messages from her mother, saying, "Good morning Sunshine, I hope you have a great, relaxing day. You deserve it," while another text from Brandon pops up stating, "Good morning, Beautiful. Cannot wait to take you out today."

Chloe steps out of the shower and puts on her pink dark robe hanging over the shower. Brushes her teeth with her electronic Colgate toothbrush and toothpaste, holding the bristles gently against the outside of her top teeth, near the gum line, at about a 45-degree angle upward. She sweeps the brush gently back and forth over her teeth in a circular motion for about two minutes, then spits into her sink twice. Grabs her Colgate mouthwash and gargles for 30 seconds. When she is done she washes her mouth out and begins to wash her face with Shea Moisturizer Scrub. Rinses her face by putting both hands under the water and splashing it on her face while she is leaning over the sink. Chloe dries her face and body with her Hammam Turkish beige towel. Then hears a knock at the door.

Mya: Knock, knock, Chloe.

Chloe: Come in, Mya. (*Chloe has her towel wrapped around her.*)

Mya: So, what is Ms. Chloe doing up so early on her day off?

Chloe: Well, if you must know (*jokingly*), I am going on a date with . . .

Mya: Brandon? The man you met at Hole in the Wall Cafe?

Chloe: Yes.

Mya: Oh wow ! What made you say yes? Especially being that it's only been three months since you know who. Have you fully healed from that?

Chloe: I believe I have. I will not sit around feeling sorry for myself. I can't meet who God has for me if I do not try.

Episode 3: Courtship

Mya: You're right. However, you cannot fully invest into a relationship or someone else until you have fully invested in yourself. Your self-healing, spirituality, etc.

Chloe: I believe I have.

Mya: Well hey, go for it.

Chloe: He should be here in the next hour.

Mya: What are you wearing? (*She sits on Chloe's bed.*)

Chloe: Its brunch, so I'll just wear one of my sun dresses.

Mya: Okay, well I'll let you get yourself together. (*Getting up off Chloe's bed, walking towards the door.*)

Chloe: I'll tell you when I'm done so you can see the final result.

Mya: Alright. I'll be in my room.

Chloe proceeds to her vanity and sits down to put on some light makeup. She feels it to be unnecessary to put on a full face. She puts on her favorite red lipstick, some blush, mascara, and eyeliner. She goes into her closet (*still wrapped in her towel*) and looks through her sundresses hanging up. Finally grabs her sun dress that is a floral print, cottage core, A-line, backless, chest lace-up, ruffled chest, spaghetti strap/short puff sleeve, high waist, slim fit, elegant midi dress. Grabs her vintage leather jacket and her open-tie crisscross self-tie heels. Puts on her Michael Kors rose gold watch.

Chloe: (*Yells out*) Mya, come here, love.

Mya: (*Rushes into the room.*) Girl yes! You look so good! What purse are you taking?

Chloe: My little brown Michael Kors purse.

Mya: Perfect. You should wear your solid brown straw hat. (*Mya grabs it off Chloe's hat rack behind her door.*)

Chloe: Thanks, Mya!

Mya: No worries!

Chloe: (*Looks at her phone and receives a text*) He said he will be here in 5 minutes. He's really on time.

Episode 3: Courtship

Mya: As he should be! Send me the address of where you guys are going and send me your location, so I'll know where you are at all times.

Chloe: So extra. (*Begins to laugh as she's sending everything to Mya.*)

Mya: Well, some of these men are extra crazy. You never know! We gotta be safe!

Chloe: I know! (*Doorbell rings.*)

Mya: Oh shoot! I'll go get the door for you, lift your boobs up and put some more lipstick on.

Chloe: (*Laughs.*) Okay. Thank you!

Mya goes down the stairs. Opens the door and sees Brandon standing there, flawless caramel skin, beautiful pearly white smile, dark brown eyes, hair full of waves, and a nice clean goatee, broad shoulders, muscular arms, 5' 11". A lime green solid shirt and matching pocket front shorts with white Vans. Holding flowers in his hand.

Mya: Well, hello there, Brandon. What time do you plan to have my friend back home?

Brandon: (*Laughs.*) You must be Mya?

Mya: The one and only. So, what time will you have her back?

Brandon: (*Smiles.*) We will be back by 6 pm or sooner.

Mya: Okay, and just so you know, she will be sharing her location with me, so be good to her! (*Chloe walks down the stairs with her hair in a beautiful high bun.*)

Brandon: Oh wow! Chloe, you look beautiful!

Chloe: (*Smiles with her teeth.*) Aww thank you! Are those sunflowers for me?

Brandon: (*As he hands them to her.*) Yes, they sure are.

Mya: Here Chloe let me take those for you. I'll put them in water. Have fun! Remember, Brandon, I have her location!

Episode 3: Courtship

    Brandon and Chloe laugh, and Brandon says, "I got her, Mya!"

Brandon: Are you ready?

    Chloe says, "Yes." Brandon walks her to his 2015 silver Porsche and opens the passenger door. Chloe gets in and Brandon closes her door and gets into the driver seat. He smiles at Chloe and starts the car engine and says, "Let's get this day started." As they're driving, Brandon says, "Are you ready for my playlist? I should've been a DJ."

Chloe: Oh, really now?

Brandon: Yes, really!

Chloe: How about we make things more interesting?

Brandon: What are we talking, Ms. Chloe?

Chloe: How about if I do not enjoy your playlist you have to wear whatever I tell you to on our next date?

Brandon: Oh! Our next date? Okay, thinking ahead already.

Chloe laughs as Brandon pushes shuffle on his phone and the first song comes on by Soul For Real called "Candy Rain." As soon as the beat drops Chloe smirks and Brandon says, "Uh huh, got her!" Chloe laughs and they both begin singing the lyrics as they're laughing and moving to the beat.

Brandon: Okay, now watch what I got next. He pushes next on his steering wheel.

Chloe hears the instrumental and says, "No you did not! I love this song! Bryson Tiller!" She begins singing the words to this popular song. Brandon begins to laugh with Chloe.

Brandon: Oh, I see I gotta watch out for Bryson Tiller. I see he's my competition now.

Chloe: Maybe. No, I am just playing with you. I do enjoy his music though.

Brandon: I do too! Okay, one more song. We are almost at the restaurant. I know you will love it!

Episode 3: Courtship

Chloe: Okay, let's hear it.

The song "Lord Your Grace," by Fred Hammond comes on, and they both begin to sing together again about the goodness and the abundant mercy of the Lord.

Chloe: This is literally one of my favorite songs, Brandon.

Brandon: Mine too! It gives me peace. One of the songs I really listen to when I am going through things, you know.

Chloe: Yes, I know. To know His love and grace is everything to me. I would not know what to do without it!

Brandon pulls into the parking lot. "I'm growing to get back there. Well, we made our Karaoke session, and it has ended (*laughing*). I also do not have to wear what you want me to wear on our next date." Chloe laughs while Brandon gets out of the car to open her door. He then says jokingly, "You know what I would love to see what you would like me to wear." Chloe says, "I am ready to give you some sense of style," and they begin to walk closer towards the restaurant and Brandon walks up to the host.

Brandon: Good morning, my name is Brandon and I have reservations for 11:00 am.

Host: Okay, let me check. Awesome! Would you like outdoor seating or inside ?

Brandon: What would you like, Chloe?

Chloe: Outside is fine. It's beautiful out.

Host: Right this way.

Chloe and Brandon follow the host to their seats outside right next to the sidewalk where you could see the street. Brandon pulls out Chloe's chair and she sits down. The host puts menus on the table and Brandon then sits down.

Host: Your waiter will be right with you.

Brandon and Chloe: Thank you!

Brandon: So, Chloe, tell me why you finally decided to go on a date with me.

Episode 3: Courtship

Chloe: I mean we have been talking for a while now. So why not? Plus, I really do enjoy our conversations and your ambition as well.

Waitress: Hello, my name is Jane, and I will be serving you today. What could I get you two started with?

Chloe: Well, I would like a mimosa.

Waitress: What flavor?

Chloe: May I have mango please.

Waitress: Yes, and you sir ?

Brandon: You know what? I will have the same.

Waitress: Alright I'll get those orders in for you both.

Brandon: Chloe, is this your first time here?

Chloe: Yes, it is. So what's good to eat here?

Brandon: I love their omelets. You can actually build your own.

Chloe: Okay, whatever omelet you get I'll get that too.

Brandon: Sounds good.

Chloe: So, serious question?

Brandon: Uh-oh! She is about to get deep on me. (*Laughs.*) No, but go ahead ask me anything.

Chloe: In the car you said you are trying to get your faith back to where it used to be. What do you mean by that? Do you still believe?

Brandon: Um... great question. I do still believe but there are some things I went through in the church that have me wanting to just do me. I can do church at home.

Waitress: Here are your drinks.

Chloe: Oooh... looks good.

Waitress: So, what will you two be eating?

Episode 3: Courtship

Brandon: We'll both have the smothered breakfast burrito, a first for us.

Waitress: With everything on it?

Brandon: Chloe is that okay?

Chloe: Yes, everything you are having.

Waitress: Alright. I'll get that in for you guys.

Chloe and Brandon: Thank you!

Chloe: So, I know we can have church anywhere but fellowship with people of God is so needed.

Brandon: I hear you but some people in the church are worse than the ones in the world.

Chloe: I totally understand.

Brandon: Church hurt is real.

Chloe: It definitely is! I have some myself. So, I will make sure to be in prayer for your healing from that. Maybe next week you can come to my church Bible study.

Brandon: I am open to that.

Waitress: Here is your food. Be careful; the plates are really hot. Would you two like another mimosa?

Brandon and Chloe: Sure, thank you.

Chloe: Do you mind praying over the food?

Brandon: Sure.

Brandon and Chloe bow their heads as Brandon begins to pray "Heavenly Father, thank you for bringing us here today to get to know one another. Bless our food to be a nourishment to our bodies, no sickness or disease to come upon us, and bless the hands that prepared it. Keep us safe and under your protection the rest of the day. Thank you Lord. In Jesus name, Amen!

Chloe: Amen!

Episode 3: Courtship

Brandon: Alright! Let's eat! You are going to love it!

Chloe looks at the food and says, "Wow! It looks great! Smells amazing too!" Chloe and Brandon both get their napkins and put it on their laps. Both of them grab their forks and begin to eat.

Brandon: What do you think ? (*After he swallows his first bite.*)

Chloe: I am not even going to lie; it is so great! That flavor is amazing! (*As she's eating.*)

Brandon: Stick with me, Shortie. We will always eat good!

Chloe: I believe it!

Brandon: So, did you want to go to the zoo or bowling?

Chloe: Honestly, I'd rather go bowling.

Brandon: I kind of had a feeling you did! I think we will have more fun there anyway!

Chloe: Agreed! How about if you lose you have to come to Bible study with me next Wednesday.

Brandon: Okay, bet! If you lose, our next date will be a hot air balloon.

Chloe: You know I told you I am afraid of heights!

Brandon: (*Laughs.*) I know!

Chloe: (*Laughs.*) You're not right! But okay, bet!

Brandon: Great! I am about to win; you know that's right!

Chloe: Do not let my shortness fool you, my little arms have some strength!

Waitress: Are you two okay? Do you need anything?

Chloe: May I just have a glass of water, please?

Brandon: May I have the check, please. I did not realize it is almost 12:30 pm!

Episode 3: Courtship

Waitress: You're enjoying yourself! I'll get that check for you!

Brandon: Thank you, Ma'am! But okay, Chloe; we shall see! So, what was your life like growing up? I know you told me your parents got divorced when you were 13 years old and remarried when you were 18. How was that for you?

Chloe: It was hard you know, in my teen years. I wished they lived together. But I got used to it. My parents did well with coparenting. Of course, I was overjoyed for them to be remarried. It was truly a blessing and something I prayed for.

Brandon: That's beautiful! Well, my dad was in and out of my life and we are growing our relationship back now. My parents were never married. My mom was a nurse and she made sure me and my sibling participated in many activities, and of course, she made sure we were at church.

Chloe: Your mom sounds amazing! How often do you talk to your dad?

Brandon: She truly is! We talk at least once a week now.

Waitress: Here's your check, sir. You both have a beautiful rest of your day.

Brandon: Thank you! You as well.

Chloe: I am happy to hear that you're back talking to your father! So, what are your views on marriage?

Brandon: I believe marriage is beautiful! It is something I want but do not want to rush into, being that marriage is sacred. It needs to be on God's timing is what I mean by not to rush. I believe some people just like the look of marriage, but do not fully understand what marriage truly is. Making sure the relationship is authentic. Both parties understand their responsibilities — the husband as well as the wife. The woman truly understands what it means to accept the man's last name, as well as the man understanding the responsibility to protect and provide for his woman.

Chloe: I definitely agree with you! Especially with God's timing and Him being in the center!

Brandon: Let's talk more about this when we go bowling! You got the check, right?

Episode 3: Courtship

Chloe: Yeah! Sure.

Brandon: I am just playing with you, girl (*Both start laughing hysterically.*)

Chloe: I know you were joking. Let's go!

Brandon and Chloe get back to the car and Google the nearest bowling alley, called Striking It.

Chloe: (*When they arrive at the bowling alley*) Darn! We don't have socks.

Brandon: It's cool. I got you! We can buy some here! What size shoe do you wear?

Chloe: A size 6.

Brandon: Little shortie (*Laughs and goes up to the counter.*)

Employee at the counter: (*Had green eyes, Caucasian, and in his early 20s.*) What can I do for you?

Brandon: May I have a size thirteen, and a size six in women?

Employee: Here you go! How many hours would you like to play?

Brandon: Chloe is an hour fine?

Chloe: Yes, cool with me!

Brandon: An hour please, sir.

Employee: Okay, you two will be on lane #5.

Brandon: Also, where can I buy some socks?

Employee: Over by the arcade.

Brandon: Alright, thanks brotha.

Chloe and Brandon walk towards the arcade. There aren't many people in the bowling alley because usually on Saturdays people come to this particular bowling alley for cosmic bowling. So, it turned out to be more intimate so they could actually talk. Brandon gives Chloe her socks after he buys them from the vending machine. They then walk to their bowling lane and begin putting on their socks and bowling shoes.

Brandon: Alright Dr. Chloe, get ready to get spanked.

Chloe: Do not be so confident, sir!

Brandon begins typing in their names and puts his name as the "Crusher" and Chloe's as "I Tried."

Chloe: You are something else, homeboy. (*Begins laughing.*)

Chloe is up first, and she is holding a pink, 8-pound bowling ball. Her form is almost perfect. She rolls the bowling ball and hits all but one pin!

Brandon: Oh, shoot! You are good! (*With a big smile on his face.*)

Chloe: I told you, Mr. Crusher! (*Chloe grabs her ball and rolls again and gets the last pin!*)

Brandon: (*Gets up and grabs a blue 12-pound bowling ball.*) Alright, Dr. Chloe. Let me show you what a strike looks like. (*Brandon rolls the bowl and he actually makes a strike! Chloe's mouth drops!*)

Chloe: Okay, I see you!

Brandon: Uh-huh!

Chloe: It's all good!

Chloe and Brandon are neck and neck through the whole game and Brandon wins by one pin.

Chloe: I guess you win huh?

Brandon: Yes, so we are going to overcome your fear and get in that hot air balloon.

Chloe: Oh, Lord!

Brandon: You'll be fine. I also will be fine to attend your Bible study next week!

Chloe: But I lost.

Episode 3: Courtship

Brandon: I know but I want to go with you.

Chloe: Aww, you are sweet.

Brandon: So are you!

Chloe: Corn ball!

Brandon: I'm serious! I am looking forward to more time with you.

Chloe: I am too.

Brandon: Are you ready to go home?

Chloe: No, but I really need to rest before clinicals. I am almost there! Speaking of my career. What made you step into your career of being an architect? (*As they are both changing back into their shoes.*)

Brandon: Well, I used to always build and create when I was younger. Legos were my everything. My mom will be the first one to tell you Legos were my life! As I got older I met friends in high school and people from different countries in college who struggled with housing. I thought to myself how cool would it be to build schools, houses, and businesses for those in need, you know?

Chloe: Wow! That is really cool!

Brandon: What about you? Did you always want to be a doctor?

Chloe: No, I actually wanted to be a teacher. It wasn't until my close friend in high school, and still till this day lost her baby sister. The doctors could not find out what was wrong with her! She was always throwing up, having seizures, and headaches, and they just could not help her. That made me want to become a doctor.

Brandon: I am sorry to hear about your friend's sister.

Chloe: Yeah, I miss her every day! That is why I have to make sure I maintain my focus!

Brandon: Well, let's get you home!

Brandon and Chloe arrive at Chloe's home. Brandon opens her car door and walks her to the door.

Episode 3: Courtship

Brandon: I really enjoyed you today.

Chloe: I enjoyed you too. I had a lot of fun!

Brandon: Next, time for a hot air balloon, right?

Chloe: Yes, and I'll see you next Wednesday at Bible study?

Brandon: I will be there! (*Brandon kisses Chloe on the cheek.*) Have a great rest of your day, Beautiful.

Chloe: (*Blushes.*) You too.

Chloe walks into the house and closes the door with her back against it, holding the knob, and says to herself with a smile "Man, I really like him."

Episode 4: PLAYING WITH FIRE

It is now the end of October and Chloe and Brandon have been hitting it off great! Dates upon dates. Chloe has even been staying the night at Brandon's house some nights. One of those nights got really heated. Brandon begins touching on Chloe and moving his hand down Chloe's leggings. Her breath begins to go harder.

Chloe: Brandon, stop. I can't.

Brandon: I'm sorry! I know you're waiting.

Chloe: Don't be sorry. I'm the one that is staying the night. You cannot play with fire. I am going to go ahead and head home.

Brandon: Are you sure? I can sleep on the couch.

Chloe: No, it's fine. I think it is better I go home.

Brandon: Okay, but please call me when you get home.

Chloe: I will.

Episode 4: Playing with Fire

Brandon opens the front door and walks Chloe outside, opens her car door, and kisses her on her forehead and says, "Again, be safe and call me when you get home." Chloe smirks and says, "Got it!" Chloe pulls out of the driveway and the song by Monica called, "The First Night," begins to play on her Apple playlist. Chloe laughs and says to herself, "Wow! Really? Out of all the songs to come on right now!" Chloe begins to think of how close she came to having sex and allowing Brandon to touch her the way he did. When she pulls up to her house so does Mya.

Mya: (*Gets out of her car.*) Girl, where have you been?

Chloe: Girl, at Brandon's. (*As she is grabbing her suitcase out of the car.*)

Mya: Girl, let's talk!

Chloe: (*Laughs.*) Yes girl, lets!

Chloe's cell phone begins to ring. Chloe looks at her phone screen and says, "He was not playing when he said to call him when I made it home." Chloe answers the phone.

Brandon: Did you make it?

Chloe: Yes, I literally just walked through the door with Mya.

Brandon: Good! And tell Mya hi.

Chloe: Will do.

Brandon: Well, have a good night! I will catch up with you this week.

Chloe: Sounds good.

Brandon: And Chloe...

Chloe: Yes?

Brandon: (*Nervously*) I (*clears throat*).. I love you.

Chloe: (*Pauses.*) Oh wow. I care a lot about you too. Why do you think you love me?

Mya: (*Shouts out from upstairs.*) Chloe, I'm coming, give me just a minute.

Episode 4: Playing with Fire

Chloe: (*Tells Brandon*) Actually, can we talk about this tomorrow?

Brandon: Yes, go ahead and spend time with Mya. I will make sure to hit you up this week. Have a great night, Beautiful.

Chloe: You too!

Mya: (*Comes down the stairs.*) Girl, you're smiling pretty hard.

Chloe: I know!

Chloe and Mya laugh and sit on the couch

Mya: So, talk to me. What has been going on? We both have been so busy, and you are barely here anymore. Have you had sex? (*Giving Chloe a serious look.*)

Chloe: No, but we were so close tonight! He just told me he loved me on the phone right before you came downstairs.

Mya: Girl! No, you were not! And no, he didn't say he loved you! Did he give you reasons why?

Chloe: Yes, we did! He was touching me a lot, but I stopped him. No, he hasn't told me why yet but we're going to talk about it this week.

Mya: No disrespect; I know you're waiting until marriage, but in this generation you know that is extremely hard to do. Especially being that he has his own space and so do you.

Chloe: I can't miss what I have never had. Plus, I believe it can be done if there are boundaries in place.

Mya: Well, you spending the night over there is not a boundary, and it is not fair to an experienced man.

Chloe: Yeah. I know, so I'm going to cut back from going over there.

Mya: Girl you are grown and if you guys plan to stay together what is the harm? As long as you guys are using protection you're good. I know you are a Christian but girl, you are human too.

Episode 4: Playing with Fire

Chloe: I know, but is it worth it? Was losing your virginity worth it?

Mya: Actually no. But I know what I like now and what I don't like. You have to test drive.(*Starts laughing.*)

Chloe: Why test drive though? If my husband will be the only one, I'm going to think he's the best because I won't have anything to compare it to.

Mya: Girl, all I'm saying is if you do decide to have sex don't beat yourself about it.

Chloe: I'll just wait.

Mya: (*Laughs.*) Good luck, girl. Let's get ready for bed because we both got to work in the morning.

Chloe: I'm going to journal then go to bed.

Mya: Alright, goodnight. Don't stay up too late. Don't think too deeply.

Chloe: I won't.

Chloe and Mya both head upstairs to their own rooms. Chloe finds her, "You're Worth More," journal and begins to write a prayer.

"God, first and foremost, thank You for always loving me. I give You praise for allowing me to even have the air to breathe and the things You have blessed me and my family with. Forgive me for my fleshly desires. If Brandon is the one for me, Lord please reveal it to me. Let me not be a distraction for his purpose or vice versa. Let me be an example of who You really are, not only physically, but mentally and emotionally. You are not just God. You are a comforter and a friend. God, let me be a vessel in the way you have called me to be. Please keep me from my own selfish desires. Father, bless me to be a whole woman of God, that my heart is so wrapped in You that he has to seek You first in order to get to me.

Thank You for allowing me to understand what it actually means to be a Proverbs 31 woman. Thank you, Lord, for allowing me to keep my focus on the vision You have for my life. Thank You for helping him to be the whole man of God You have called him to be. Let him seek Your face in all things. No matter how he may feel or how things may look, let him trust You! Bless his dreams to be Your dreams and Your ways to become his ways. In Jesus' name, Amen!

Love,

Your Daughter,

Chloe

The next Monday Chloe calls Brandon during her lunch break. She receives no answer. It is now Friday and still no word from him. When Chloe is getting ready to end her shift she goes into the residence conference room and see's Patrice. Chloe gives Patrice a fake smile. Patrice notices something is wrong.

Patrice: Chloe, you okay? I know it has been a little tough this week. But we're almost there to live out our dream jobs.

Chloe: Yes, I am okay.

Patrice: Are you sure? Because you gave me that fake little smirk of a smile.

Chloe: (*Laughs.*) You know what! I am not okay. Brandon has not called me all week. The last time we spoke he told me he loved me, and we were going to talk about it the next day.

Patrice: Well Chloe, you know I say actions speak louder than words.

Chloe: What if something happened to him?

Patrice: You have met some of his close friends and family haven't you?

Chloe: Yes, but I am not super close to them yet.

Patrice: Whether you are close or not, if something happened to Brandon and they know you two are serious, they'll reach out to let you know.

Chloe: Well, what if there's just a lot going on in his life or something?

Patrice: Stop making excuses for him. If something is going on, he is an adult and can communicate that with you. Chloe, you are in your last year of residency. You have a lot going on as well. And honestly you do not have time trying to guess if a man is still interested. You have to focus.

Josh walks in. "Well, hello ladies."

Episode 4: Playing with Fire

Patrice: Oh Gosh! I will call you later, Chloe.

Chloe: Alright. See you guys later.

Joshua: Really? I want to have a girl talk too.

Chloe and Patrice: Bye Josh!

Joshua: (*Looks at himself in the glass window.*) They both know they want me.

SEASON FINALE

Chloe: How did I get here? (*Chloe begins thinking back to how she and Brandon even met. Her heart is pounding, and she is extremely nervous.*)

Brandon comes out of his room, eager to get back to Chloe. Brandon says, "Sorry it took me so long. I couldn't find them. It has been so long." Brandon grabs Chloe's face to his and begins kissing her passionately. As he's kissing her he lays her back on the couch and rips the condom open with his mouth.

Chloe: Brandon. You know what? I can't do this. I have to go. I would rather wait. I'm sorry, but I have to go.

Brandon: (*As Chloe is putting back on her clothes and gathering her things*) Chloe you don't have to leave. We can just talk. I'm sorry.

Chloe: (*Walking towards the door*) It isn't your fault I have to go.

Brandon: Chloe, please don't go.

Chloe dashes out the door. She puts her things away in the car while Brandon is just watching her. She closes her trunk, gets into the car and starts her engine. Brandon watches her drive away and says to himself "I can't lose her."

As Chloe is driving home she calls Patrice. The phone rings three times.

Patrice: (*Picks up the phone.*) Hey Chloe, what's up?

Chloe: Can you come to my place? I need you and Mya right now.

Patrice: Yes, of course! Are you okay?

Chloe: Yes, I am fine. I just need some wisdom.

Patrice: Okay, give me 30 minutes and I'll be over there.

Chloe: Okay, thank you so much!

Patrice: Always! See you in a minute. Bye.

Chloe: Bye.

Chloe pulls up to her house and walks inside and sees Mya on the couch.

Mya: Hey, girl! What's up? I'm almost caught up with you on the Vampire Diaries series.

Chloe: (*Laughs a little bit.*) Finally huh?

Mya: Yes, it is getting good too!

Chloe: I am glad you are up. I am going to shower and put on some pajamas, and I'll be back down. I need to talk to you, and Patrice is coming over too.

Mya: Are you good?

Chloe: Yes, just give me like 30 minutes.

Mya: Alright. I'll be up watching Vampire Diaries.

Chloe laughs and walks up the stairs. She gets into the shower right away. She washes her body down with Dove Unscented soap. She begins to think back of how close she was to having sex with Brandon. Thinking to herself, "I made the right decision, right? Am I overthinking this?" Chloe steps out of the shower and grabs her pink robe. She dries herself off and grabs her Shea Moisture to lotion down her body. She puts on her Paris Hilton perfume and grabs some pink striped pajamas.

Mya: (*Shouts out.*) Chloe, Patrice just got here!

Chloe: Okay, just a second.

Chloe says out loud to herself "So grateful for genuine friends." She then puts on her pink slippers and heads downstairs. Patrice hugs Chloe and says, "Now girl, you know I had to bring two bottles of this Stella Rosa Black wine. Now tell me what is going on."

Mya: I love you, Patrice. Always got the wine on deck.

They all begin to laugh, and Patrice goes into the kitchen and starts pouring each of them a glass.

Patrice: Well, go ahead and tell us what is going on.

Mya: Yeah! Come on spill it.

Chloe: I almost had sex with Brandon tonight. I left when he got the condom.

Mya: Girl, you left that man with blue balls? That's not right!

Patrice: She has a right to say she does not want to have sex.

Mya: Yes, she does but don't go that far knowing you are not going to. That isn't okay!

Patrice: Look Chloe, you didn't want to have sex and that is okay. However, going to his home and expecting things not to happen? You have to set boundaries.

Chloe: You're right.

Mya: Lets be real. You want to have sex. You are almost thirty.

Chloe: Yeah. I'm human. Of course I do. But I think it's worth waiting for.

Patrice: Then set the boundaries, Boo. Set boundaries.

Mya: And stop playing with that man!

Patrice: I just think you two should talk and go over some boundaries. Do not make him out to be the bad guy.

Chloe: I know. I'll just wait and talk to him tomorrow. (*There is a knock on the door.*)

Patrice: Y'all expecting someone?

Mya says no and gets up from the couch and goes to the door. A look of shock comes over her face when she looks through the peephole. Looks at Chloe and says, "It's Brandon."

Chloe: What! Really? (*Chloe gets up and opens the door.*)

Brandon: Hey.

Chloe: Hey.

AUTHOR'S BIOGRAPHICAL SKETCH

 Areva Denise Neely was born in Santa Monica, California and raised in Moreno Valley, California. She holds a Bachelor's Degree in Business Administration and a Master's Degree in Educational Leadership from California Baptist University. She is currently working on a Master's in School Counseling.

Areva is the author of three books — *You're Worth More, Intentionally Seeking,* and *Blossoming Nicely.* These books share her personal testimony to help other young women to know their worth spiritually and naturally. Besides being an author, Areva is a youth minister, mentor, motivational speaker, optimal health educator, soon to be school counselor, and business owner.

During the pandemic of 2020, Areva opened the Little Inspirations Tutoring Program to enable parents to work while their children had a safe space to do schoolwork, have Bible study, and make friends. Areva's main goal is to open a youth center in her city to inspire the youth to live out their purpose. She wants young people to exemplify their talents without compromising their values, while obtaining a higher education.

AUTHOR'S CONTACT INFORMATION

Email - IllJustWait25@gmail.com

Website -

https://arevadenise.wixsite.com/arevadenise/about

Twitter - @areva_denise

Instagram - @areva_denise

Phone - (951)796-0282

Made in the USA
Monee, IL
03 January 2023

20534492R00069